Road
Kill

Tina Hill

DEDICATION

Mr. Calvin L. McJunkins
(Rest in peace dear friend)

CONTENTS

ACKNOWLEDGMENTS

A special thanks to Victoria Clifford and Wilbert Mathews
for your invaluable suggestions and comments.

CHAPTER ONE

'At night Old Mill Road is deserted . . . strange chills drift on the air . . . the quaking pines whisper . . .'

The exaggerations about Pine Hollow's murders filled her thoughts as Lori siphoned the gas from Beth's tank. When the serial killings started happening two years ago, they fast became the subject of creepy speculation. As the murders continued to happen and word spread, reality flew out the window. Now detecting the truth would stump even Sherlock Holmes.

Next, someone will write a folksong . . .

Focus on draining the tank, Lori ordered herself.

How much longer will it take? She suddenly lost her patience. She had been standing there nearly half an hour transferring Beth's gas into the company's utility vehicle. She'd watched her dad siphon gas from his pickup truck into his lawn equipment in only a few minutes. Soon, someone at the picnic would notice her absence.

Look around you. Make sure no one's coming.

Her gaze swept the Hamilton Mills' parking garage entrance. No one had driven in or out since she'd been there, but at any moment someone invited to the picnic could show up and spot her.

1

Ordinarily, only the company emergency vehicles parked on the first floor. Today, since upper level space was limited because of the company picnic, Jared had let Beth and Lori park their cars on the entrance level.

Bloody knife glistening . . .

Without warning, an image from an embellished version of the slayings stood before her eyes.

Think about something else Lori told herself. Look around you. Concentrate on your surroundings. Watch the lush green pine forest sway in the hot midday sun. Listen to the bob white call out his name to the woods. See the green lizard changing colors as it scurries along the russet beam above Beth's car. Inhale the clean forest air.

But no matter how hard she tried to erase the gory mental picture and admire the Northwest scenery around her, the bloody knife remained before her eyes.

Lori dropped her gaze and watched the gas rush through the siphon hose: Flowing like blood—

Sudden doubt grabbed her.

Maybe she shouldn't do this. Maybe some sixth sense was warning her to stop it. If anyone ever learned that she had drained Beth's tank, she could spend the rest of her life in prison.

She wouldn't do it.

She would stop the transfer right now. She would put on a smile, go back to the picnic, and make sure things there were going well. When she started dating again, she would find a man interested in no one but her.

Lori reached a hand out to stop the gas flow, but memory of the humiliation and betrayal that had led her to this point stopped her mid-reach. She remembered the heaviness always centered in her chest, the brain fog that clouded her thinking. Most of all, she remembered the smirk, the smirk that went back to her childhood. The smirk Beth Hines now put on her face whenever Lori Manning came in sight.

Her memory traveled back to a hot summer afternoon:

Two little girls sitting outside on the porch swing eating strawberry Popsicles while their mothers were inside visiting.

The little girl Lori wanted her Popsicle to last. She slowly enjoyed its icy sweetness. Little girl Beth lapped up hers then demanded Lori's Popsicle.

"No," Lori refused.

Beth tumbled off the swing then ran inside the house screaming, "Lori took my Popsicle."

"Give Beth her Popsicle." Both mothers stood at the door.

Tears streamed down her cheeks as the words of denial locked in her throat.

Lori shoved her Popsicle into Beth's hands. Beth ran back to the porch swing slurping the Popsicle, smirking.

The hurt and rage Lori had felt as that little girl now resurfaced. Memory of her mother's lecture: 'Never take things that don't belong to you' at once renewed her determination.

No.

No way would she stop the siphoning. Lori withdrew her hand.

Time had come to teach Beth a lesson. If Beth got away with her most recent theft, it would validate her belief that she could take anything she wanted. If Lori backed out now, Beth would forever see her as the powerless little girl who'd lost her Popsicle, her two high school boyfriends, and then the man she loved to Beth. If she didn't fight for what she wanted today and then regretted it tomorrow, she would have to wait a year until the next picnic for another opportunity.

Every six months a woman stranded alone at night on Old Mill Road was murdered. Six months had passed since the last one. If all the fates came together, the next murder would happen tonight.

To Beth, no one deserved to die more.

Sprawled lifeless at the bottom of the gorge alongside

the road, throat slit, her personal items missing. Just like the others.

Death chills the air . . .

The tales would blossom.

Lori tossed back a lock of her ash-brown hair and again scanned the garage entrance; still no one in sight. She glanced over her shoulder: The stately pine forest rippled. The only sound came from cooing doves.

While Lori watched Beth's gas flow, her thoughts strayed. The whole town knew James Jefferson Cooper was the serial killer. However, Sheriff Tate and Bexar County Homicide Investigators had found no evidence that proved it.

Not surprising, Tate wasn't the sharpest knife in the kitchen.

Jimmy Jay Cooper owned the one service station on Old Mill Road between Pine Hollow and Pine Ridge thirty miles south. At night stuffed behind the wheel of his big black tow truck, he wandered the county roads looking for loggers and motorists having vehicle trouble. Jimmy thought it was funny to turn off the headlights then creep up on them in the dark like a big black cricket.

Again, Lori pictured the knife he would use:

Long steel blade . . . moonlight reflecting off the razor sharp edges . . .

The same one he'd used to kill the others.

CHAPTER TWO

James J. Cooper inched along in line at the Hamilton Mills Annual Company Picnic regretting that he'd skipped breakfast. Had he known he would have to wait so long for lunch he would've eaten a bowl of cereal this morning. By now, he would be hungry enough again to enjoy all the picnic food he wanted. For the last forty-five minutes, he'd crept along in the line toward the tables. Now the smell of smoked pork ribs, beef brisket, and barbecued chicken taunted his hunger.

His patience wearing thin Jimmy glanced over his shoulder. The line behind him now stretched outside the tarp-covered food area, past the tables under the trees, almost to the garage.

His stomach grumbled as he turned back to the food-laden tables.

Every year Hamilton Mills, the local company that kept the small town in existence, held a picnic that brought out most of Pine Hollow's residents. Jimmy knew the picnic arrangements by heart. Six double rows of folding tables topped by every picnic food imaginable stood centered beneath the block long tarp cover staked on company grounds. Along the tarp's outer edges, more long tables arranged in a U-shape stretched the width and length of the tent. Folding chairs provided seating at the tables. White plastic tablecloths covered the surface tops. Later, a Hamilton Mills representative would raffle off the large floral centerpieces.

Across the lawn, on a corner of the parking lot, a rock country band Jimmy had managed to tune-out until now worked on his nerves. As the assault on his ears grew louder, the disdain on his face deepened. Jimmy turned his gaze in the band's direction. A hip-wiggling male singer dressed in a beaded and sequined western outfit strummed a guitar and screamed above the blast of the drums, *Like a Rhinestone Cowboy.*

More like the *Dance of the Sugar Plum Fairy* Jimmy muttered under his breath and then turned back to the tables.

"James Cooper, I haven't seen you in ages. How have you been?"

The sound of his name lifted above the din of the music. Jimmy scanned the maze of people, tables, running and yelling kids for the source of the female voice. His search landed on Anne Johnson heading toward him, smiling.

"Okay," Jimmy mumbled through a mouthful of coconut cake he had eased from the nearby dessert table. He couldn't resist diving into it while he waited to fill his plates.

"Jimmy, are you ever coming back to church? How long has it been?" Anne asked.

He shrugged embarrassed that he couldn't remember and that she had caught him with his mouth full. He hoped white coconut flakes didn't litter his red beard. He had brushed off what had fallen on the front of his blue cover-ups.

"Come back to church sometime, Jimmy, we miss that beautiful voice."

Jimmy grinned then glanced over the area. Every eye

there was on him. All at once, he felt important. The whole town knew that Anne's husband was a successful attorney. Until she walked up, everybody he'd nodded to had looked the other way. No one had acknowledged his presence. Now he was the center of attention.

"Jimmy Jay, glad you came out," Jared Bolton walked over and slapped Jimmy's shoulder. "Nice to see you're wearing our company logo cap. It fits you well. Help yourself to the food. Don't be shy. Take as much as you want." Jared's left hand rested on Jimmy's shoulder.

Jimmy cast a quick glance at Beth Hines standing next to Jared not smiling or saying a word to anyone. Not even to Anne. Beth and Lori Manning used to be best friends, thought Jimmy.

"Take care, Jimmy. If you ever need anything, Greg and I are here for you." Anne headed for a nearby table to rejoin her husband and four kids.

"Thanks," Jimmy answered both Jared's and Anne's comments. At the same time, he tried not to flinch from Jared's touch. Every time Jared came by the service station, he slapped Jimmy's shoulder. "Thanks for the invitation," Jimmy said politely, glad the line was moving again so he could put ribs and beef on his plate.

"See you later, Jimmy," Jared steered Beth across the lawn toward a tree-shaded table.

Jimmy followed the line.

He piled coleslaw and baked beans high in a take-away box. At the same time, he recalled that Jared dropped by the service station often. Jared filled his gas tank only when it was empty. Sometimes when he thought he would run out before he reached the station, he had Jimmy bring him gas at work.

As Jimmy stacked barbecued ribs on a second plate, sudden jealousy flared in his chest.

Jared and Lori used to date.

A few minutes ago, Jimmy had peeked at her standing a short distance away. Her lips wore a smile, but her eyes looked like thunder.

As Jimmy added potato salad, baked beans, and bread to his meal, he suddenly pictured Lori and Jared romping around in bed together. Even though he was glad they'd broken up, mental images like that still made him resentful. They used to stay out late on the weekends and then park and smooch at Lovers Leap. Jimmy knew Beth had wormed her way between them.

Now she and Jared did the same things.

Jimmy wished Lori would go out with him. He glanced to where she stood. Disappointment filled his eyes. She had left. He wondered if she went home. He'd had a crush on her since grade school. Had she been dating him, he wouldn't have traded her for Beth. The whole town knew Beth was a tramp. In high school, she slept with almost every guy in her class. A rumor once circled that she crawled in bed with him whenever she needed her car fixed. That was a lie. He wouldn't touch Beth with a ten-foot pole. She thought he'd started the rumor and hadn't spoken to him since.

Jimmy reached the beverage line then realized he couldn't carry the food and a cup of lemonade without spilling something. He set the boxes on the table then brought the cup to his lips. Gulping sounded from his throat as he swallowed the lemonade. While he drained the cup, his sights scoured the area for a last glimpse of Lori.

Jimmy finished the drink, set the cup on the table, opened his mouth, and then let out a rumbling belch. His gaze landed on a nearby table. Councilman Cecil Jones and City Treasurer Joe Barnes stared at him with disgust open on their faces.

"Up yours," Jimmy flipped them the bird.

Lori was nowhere around.

CHAPTER THREE

Finally . . .

Beth's gas stopped flowing. Lori withdrew the transfer hose; reversed the set-up. She let only half a gallon go back into the tank. Tonight on her drive home to Pine Ridge, Beth would run out of gas deep in the heart of the woods: Looming pines, menacing dark, near the site of the four murders.

The transfer completed, Lori tossed the equipment into her trunk, made a mental note to put a new one on the utility truck.

You go girl!

She congratulated herself.

The planets had aligned in her favor. So far, things had gone without a hitch. This morning Beth had backed her car into the space next to the truck. Both fuel tanks stood side-by-side.

Lori scheduled maintenance and took weekly equipment and supply inventory on the trucks so they always stood ready to respond to any logging emergency. Just last night this truck had returned from a week in-service at a forest fire. Since it still waited inspection and refueling, it held Beth's full tank.

Lori knew every piece of emergency equipment on the trucks: First Aid kits, chain saws, gas cans, siphon pumps—everything.

For weeks, she had racked her brain for a way to get Beth out of the picture:

The gun accidentally discharged . . .

She stepped in front of the car . . .

Someone murdered her then ransacked the apartment . . .

All unacceptable; the truth would come out. Beth had ridiculed her to Pat and Janet, Beth's two Accounting co-workers who lived near her in Pine Ridge. Beth had laughed as she told them about the friction between her and Lori. Pat and Janet would recall that conversation and place Lori under immediate suspicion. She'd ditched the idea until she walked past Beth this morning and overheard her saying she had filled her tank on the way in to avoid stopping at a service station on the way home.

Problem solved.

Drain her gas.

Strand her alone tonight on Old Mill Road. Beth wouldn't check the fuel gauge again before she took off.

Jimmy Jay would take it from there.

Why didn't I think of it before? Lori wondered. As often as Jared ran low on gas, the solution should've jumped out at her.

Couldn't see the forest for the trees, she supposed.

While she twisted the fuel cap back on Beth's tank, Lori again checked the garage entrance. At the same time, she caught a glimpse of her face reflected in the right side door mirror. For the umpteenth time she was glad that she'd highlighted her hair. The gold streaks mixed into her natural color enhanced her tawny complexion. She knew her hazel eyes now hidden behind sunglasses, sparkled the way the stylist had said they would.

Smile; soften your expression.

Straight white teeth glistened in the mirror.

Overall, she wasn't hard to look at Lori told herself

(just as pretty as Beth). Regular jogging and workouts kept her figure in shape. She was nearly thirty, yet just as trim as she was at twenty. She still attracted her fair share of male attention.

Back to the picnic, Lori ordered herself. She turned around, scanned the foliage on the edge of the forest before her: Dash through it.

She darted past Sheriff Tate and Deputy Weston's blue cruisers parked beside her ancient sedan then sprinted across the narrow lawn that separated the garage and the forest.

So far so . . .

Brambles bit her arms as she bolted through the shrubbery. Skin smarting, temples pounding, hidden among the pines she stopped running. Hands on her hips she leaned forward; filled her lungs with pine-scented air; held then released it.

She could have crossed the garage, run along the walk, and then scrammed through the glass doors to get back to the picnic quicker, Lori caught her breath thinking. However, if Beth's empty gas tank ever came into question and investigators looked into it, those who knew she had filled her tank before the picnic would come forward. That could trigger someone's recall of seeing Lori run from the garage. Besides, the security cameras inside the building and those aimed at the rear door would record her movements.

Another deep breath then Lori continued walking. She hoped no one at the picnic had missed her so no questions would rise later.

Quails fleeing her presence broke the forest silence.

Lori sometimes walked inside the pine forest just for the heck of it. The understory vegetation thrived in a dim sunlit world far below the mid and upper stories. Grasses and shrubs flourished on a bed of needles and drew oxygen from the pine-scented environment.

She wove around sky-brushing pines then strode into

the clearing.

Beth—

At a picnic table; her back to the woods, she gazed dreamily into Jared's eyes.

Lori froze. If they saw her, they'd know to reach that point without passing them she'd cut through the garage. If someone ever discovered her role in Beth's murder, during the interrogation the prosecutor would state, 'Someone drained Beth's tank. Jared Bolton testified that he saw you walking from the direction of the garage.'

Besides that Beth was so self-centered she would think Lori was there spying on them.

Jared cupped Beth's cheeks between his palms.

Unnoticed, Lori stepped backwards into the forest. Braced against a tree, she slipped down it to the pine needle carpet.

Oh Jared . . .

How she missed his affectionate touch.

Three years ago, she fell in love with Operations Manager, Jared Bolton. Then Beth took him from her. Jared had transferred to Pine Hollow, a logging community of some ten thousand residents after the Quail Valley Lumber Mill where he worked purchased the then failing Hamilton Mills. Jared's creative reorganization skills had molded it into the now productive company. In the short time he'd been there, profits had soared. Under thirty-eight year-old Jared's leadership, the company sponsored the Pine Hollow Little League team, the Founder's Day Parade, and the Annual Citywide Picnic. An avid runner himself, Jared and the company also sponsored several annual long-and short-distance weekend runs.

Over the past two years, rumors had circled that the picnic would end because of the problems surrounding it. Not only were the slayings a concern, the truck traffic and road rage problems created by loggers as they rumbled lumber through the town from remote sawmills added to the trouble. This year, everyone was surprised when Jared decided to host the picnic onsite at the Old Mill Road location. Beautiful landscaped grounds snuggled amid rolling hills covered with towering pines.

'Even more dangerous,' employees complained when Jared announced the picnic would be there and not at their Canyon Hills Ranch location as usual, 'Dangerous even with Pine Hollow's law enforcement officers patrolling. Recently four women had lost their lives near the area.'

Lori agreed with the others but withheld her comments. At some point, everyone who attended the picnic had to travel Old Mill Road. Anyone who failed to leave when the picnic was over could be on the road alone after dark.

Today, when the idea struck her to see Beth become the killer's fifth victim, Lori mentally applauded Jared's decision. Once Beth was out of the way, he and Lori would get back together.

When Lori first started planning the picnic, Jared had told her to invite the whole town to it as usual. As she eased away to drain Beth's tank, she saw Jimmy Jay near the dessert table. Tonight, he would be out roaming the road in search of someone stranded.

CHAPTER FOUR

Jimmy flopped down on an old van seat just inside the service station garage. He grabbed the Styrofoam take-away box he'd brought from the picnic. His teeth sank into a barbecued rib. One bite ripped the meat off the bone. Red sauce dribbled down his chin then settled on his beard.

He wished he'd seen Lori again before he left the picnic. Every year she worked hard setting it up. He wondered if she went off somewhere to rest. The next time he saw her he'd tell her the food she ordered was good.

Jimmy chewed thoughtfully. He wondered if Lori could cook. His dad had often said that Jimmy's mother was a good cook. Since then whenever he sat down to a meal other than fast food, he pretended that she had cooked it. But that always reminded him of how much he missed her and how sorry he was that he had killed her. And each time he remembered, he wondered how he could love and miss someone he'd never met. As usual, he decided that somewhere deep within his psyche, guilt for causing her death still rode him.

He had never known his mother, but he'd killed her

just the same. She had died during his birth. Something called a 'breach birth'. A storm had delayed them getting to the hospital and complications had developed.

Jimmy often wondered what his life would've been like growing up had his mother been alive. Certainly, his childhood wouldn't have been as troubled. She would've taken on the whole town in his defense.

If she were living, he'd still stay with her since he was single and his dad had died.

Jimmy always pictured her in the kitchen: Soft classical music on the stereo while she baked coconut cakes and lemon meringue pies. Spaghetti and meatballs simmered on the stove; a pot roast browned in the oven. Home-cooked meals he'd only heard about as a boy.

They would talk about what went on in Pine Hollow; the murders, what everybody else talked about. He would act as if he knew little about them so she wouldn't send him to Doc Fowler for some sleeping pills. She'd think all the talk about the murders was the cause of him losing his sleep. He and all the now murdered women had attended school together. At night when things quieted down, he heard their screams. Behind his closed eyes, he saw their blood drops on the road.

Maybe if he were married not having his mother wouldn't bother him so much. His wife would make him dessert for breakfast if he wanted it.

No use dreaming about it, Jimmy hiccupped. No woman would ever marry him. He'd killed his mother. In grade school, the kids teased him about it:

What's his name?

Is it Tommie?

No, Jimmy Jay killed his mommy.

As he always did when he recalled the bullying, Jimmy wondered why the kids never liked him. Pine Hollow was a lumber town. People moved in and out often. The new kids were readily accepted; he'd lived there all his life but all anybody ever did was taunt him. Before long, the new kids joined in the bullying.

Jimmy stared at the nearly empty Styrofoam plate. He had been so hungry on the drive back to the station he'd polished off the shrimp and crabmeat potato salad, along with the baked beans and coleslaw. After he'd drunk the best lemonade he'd ever tasted at the picnic, he'd grabbed a soft drink that smelled and tasted like bananas and strawberries and stuffed it in his pocket. He'd drunk it while he ate and drove. He'd tell Bobby to have the soda delivery guy add that flavor to the soft drink machine.

Jimmy wrapped the last slice of bread around the last rib on the plate, took a bite, and then followed it with a ring of raw onion. He wished he had more. Jared had said he could have all he wanted.

He would've taken more had he known Lori wasn't still standing there watching. He had minded his manners for her. She always called him a pig to make him feel bad about his weight. He knew he was heavy and didn't need her or anyone else talking about it. The next time he saw her out somewhere or if she came by the station, he would make her give him a kiss if she didn't apologize.

Jimmy leaned back on the bench seat he'd taken out of an old van and set on cinder blocks. It served as a couch when things quieted down around there. Today, business was slow because of the picnic.

His thick legs stretched out before him Jimmy yawned then drifted into a doze.

Eyelids drooping, chin resting on his chest he pictured Lori and him parked at Lovers Leap.

Their lips move close . . .

Jimmy wandered into sleep; started dreaming. Soon, he heard echoes of the dead women's voices refusing to go out with him:

Do I look like an idiot?
Get out of my face.
Go to hell.
You're not my type.

Jimmy stirred, shifted his bulk on the seat, and then started snoring as he entered into deeper, more disturbing sleep:

Please don't kill me.

I'll do whatever you say.

Jimmy coughed then woke up, sobbing.

CHAPTER FIVE

Lori checked her watch.

Get your butt in gear . . .

Her nerves had settled; erratic heartbeat had evened.

She'd been away from the picnic much longer than she had expected. Nearly an hour had passed. On her feet, she began moving. When she stepped into the clearing again, she was a short distance past the picnic grounds and no one else was around.

Lori turned around and circled back wide in Beth and Jared's direction. Head down, painful thoughts filled her mind. She kicked a pinecone ahead of her feet. Jared wasn't the first guy she had lost to Beth Lori remembered. Beth had stolen Lori's two high school boyfriends.

Beth never got away scot-free with what she did. Lori always evened the score later. After Beth stole the second boyfriend, they'd stopped speaking. One evening, however, while Beth shopped at the mall, a well-aimed brick shattered her windshield.

Both had graduated community college when they met face-to-face as employees in the Hamilton Mills' cafeteria.

They had acted as if nothing had ever come between them. Over time, they'd renewed the friendship. They'd remained close friends until Accounting transferred Beth to a trailer office deep within the pinewoods. Soon afterward, she moved to Pine Ridge to be nearer her work location.

Beth had no genuine interest in the men she took from other women. She didn't do serious relationships. She lured men away from their wives or girlfriends just to prove she could do it then dumped them for someone else.

Bitch . . .

Jared was mine.

Each time Lori saw them together her heart broke all over again. Quick tears now stung her eyes. Stop it! Lori ordered herself. Don't start blubbering. He'll be yours again. We said if dating others didn't work out, we would get back together. Soon it will be as it was before Miss Ass entered the picture.

She took off her sunglasses, wiped her eyes.

Months past the breakup, the wound hadn't healed. She remained hopelessly in love with Jared. Making matters worse, this time Beth showed no signs of growing restless—

Cell . . .

Refocusing her attention Lori pulled the phone from her cargo pants pocket, checked the Caller ID: Beth's mother. Earlier, Lori had swiped Beth's phone so she couldn't call for help when her tank ran empty.

Lori continued walking toward Beth and Jared now leaned against the picnic table, locked in each other's arms. Neither one saw her approaching.

"Spend the weekend with me," Beth combed her fingers through his hair. "We'll go dancing."

"Can't, running in the county race tomorrow."

"You can skip it this once," Beth pouted.

Not watching where she walked Lori stepped on a twig. It snapped beneath her tennis.

Beth looked up. "There you are. You've been gone so

long I thought you were out hunting a new boyfriend."

"I've been minding my damned business. You should take a cue." Lori snapped.

"FYI, I'll be leaving soon so I'll be home when Jimmy Jay starts prowling."

"You're supposed to help with the clean-up," Lori gritted.

"Stay and help Lori. Jimmy Jay won't be a problem," Jared intervened. "I'll follow you until you're safely headed home."

CHAPTER SIX

'Kill him, Bobby, kill him. Give the bastard all you got. Show him your moves.'

Sweating and out of breath Jimmy woke from the dream, confused. As he got his bearings, his gaze darted over the room. Before he fell asleep, the station was well sunlit. Now, the inside dimness signaled late afternoon. Soon the picnic would be over.

In his sleep, he had dreamt about that day in sixth grade when he beat up Bobby Westland. Although Jimmy now sat up wide-awake, the dream remained vivid. His heart hadn't stopped jumping.

The dream often repeated itself. Each time he relived it, he woke up glad he and Bobby had settled their differences. Bobby now worked part-time at the service station to make extra money for his five kids.

As much as he wanted to, Jimmy couldn't clear the past from his thoughts: Bobby had snatched Jimmy's wallet and wouldn't give it back. That day Jimmy grew fed-up with the bullies always pestering him. His nose bled from a punch, his scraped knees showed through his torn pants.

Several guys tossed his wallet around daring him to take it back.

Right then, he decided he wouldn't take any more bullying. His dad and grandfather had urged him to fight back. They'd met with the kids' parents, but none of them would cooperate.

"Don't try to fight them all, Jimbo, only the leader. Kick his ass and the rest will leave you alone," his dad said.

That day Jimmy stopped chasing them. He didn't care if they killed him. Being dead would be better than living like this all the time.

He sized up the boys around him. Bobby, the leader took Jimmy's allowance from the wallet. Bobby never fought anyone himself. He egged the others on while he stood back and watched.

"Bobby, you take me," Jimmy challenged. "Fucking coward, I want a piece of you."

As he recalled it now, years later, Jimmy relived the same fear and breathlessness he had that day. His pulses pounded. His rapid breathing brought him close to hyperventilating. At the time, just before the fight, he had no idea where the cuss words came from. He hadn't practiced saying them. They just popped out of his mouth. As soon as he said them, his whole body shook. His legs wobbled as if they'd turned to rubber.

Bobby moseyed toward him. At least Bobby tried to swagger, but from where Jimmy stood, Bobby's legs looked like they would crater. His face had turned as white as sleet; his eyes had widened big and round.

At once, Jimmy realized Bobby was just as scared as he was. Bobby was fearless only when he called out orders and jeered from the sidelines.

Suddenly, Jimmy felt his legs strengthen. The terrified voice in his head that had said 'run' quieted.

To this day, he couldn't remember throwing any punches. He only knew that when the fight was over Bobby had a fractured right jaw.

That fight ended the bullying.

Nobody ever picked on James J. Cooper again.

Until then, he didn't even know he could fight. He'd always run. When they caught him, he cried while they beat him up. Although he was taller than most of them, he was a fraidy cat. He didn't like fights and spats. He'd rather go hunting and fishing with his dog, Pal.

Payback was a bitch.

After that fight, he settled any score he wanted to.

Throughout middle school and before he dropped out of high school, he'd taken down every guy who'd ever bullied him. He kicked some of their asses twice. Every male in town his age ran the other way when they saw him coming.

Somebody poisoned Pal.

Jimmy cried for two weeks and hadn't owned a dog since.

After he beat up their relatives and boyfriends, none of the girls would go out with him.

Now, some of those same women had turned up murdered. And everybody in town suspected he had killed them.

CHAPTER SEVEN

Lori tossed the last bag of picnic trash she and the clean-up crew had collected into the container next to the garage. The picnic had ended. The caterers had gathered their equipment and were gone. Most of the visitors had left. The grounds were back in their pristine condition.

As Jared's assistant, organizing and supervising the annual company picnic was her responsibility. She had worked hard all day long seeing that everything went smoothly. Now her feet ached. Sunburn stung her face and bared arms. She longed to go home and slip into a hot bath.

Lori walked away from the trash bin and strolled for the building. Last week she'd been afraid only a few people would show up. The location was near where the murders always happened. But the turnout had been better than in past years. Almost every resident had come out and taken part in the activities. While some people left soon after lunch, others stayed and visited. Employees and their families took full advantage of the annual day of recognition. They played volley and baseball, drank beer, and lingered.

Beth and Jared stepped from the back exit door,

24

headed for the garage.

"Great job, Lori, everybody had a good time. Enjoy the weekend," Jared said.

"Yeah, you did the best you could," Beth flashed her teeth, pursed her lips, and then rolled her eyes all in quick succession.

"Thanks, Jared. The new caterer is fantastic." Ignoring Beth (you'll get yours later), Lori accepted his compliment without taking any credit. "I'll definitely use them again."

As Jared and Beth walked away, Lori continued toward the door. Her right leg fell into a deliberate limp: Those two dumb asses had hobbled around together all day as if they had joined hips. Neither one had left the others side.

Probably peed together . . .

While Lori strolled, her thoughts strayed back to Jared's arrival at Hamilton Mills. At the time, she had recently received a long awaited promotion. The upgrade to Senior Administrative Assistant entitled her to support the Operations Manager. The new guy named to fill the long vacant position would arrive the next morning.

Admittedly, she had been more than a little nervous. It was her first assignment ever supporting someone that high up the executive ladder. She'd gained her experience working for mid-level managers. She wondered if her skills were strong enough to support a fast-paced executive position. Could she handle the demands of a seasoned older man?

After tossing all night, she had dressed carefully the next morning hoping to look professional for their first meeting. A charcoal tailored gabardine suit flattered her curves. A silk gray, red, and white striped blouse, black leather pumps, gold earrings, and a gold watch completed the outfit.

She arrived for work earlier than usual to make sure the movers had arranged her new office the way she wanted it. Then she would have a strong cup of coffee to settle her nerves before the new manager came in.

Lori unlocked the third floor office door a few steps down the hall past the elevator then flipped on the lights. She stood in the open doorway letting her eyes capture the scene. A six-foot mahogany credenza centered across a glass wall of floor-to-ceiling windows faced her. The windows looked out over the complex entrance back dropped by the lush pine forest.

A matching wood executive desk centered before the credenza faced the door where she stood. Near the left wall, two blue guest chairs she'd claimed from Surplus stood around a small black occasional table. Along the right wall, three dark wood file cabinets filled the space near the door that led into a small conference room. Five sable leather chairs surrounded the oval conference room table.

The movers had followed her diagram to the letter.

A second door past the conference room table led into the Op Manager's oversized office. That door stood open. Certain the movers or the cleaners had failed to close it Lori strode through the conference room to the office then grabbed the doorknob. The new Op sat with Charlie Goode, temporary manager in the position. Both looked up from paperwork spread on the desk before them. Both appeared annoyed by the intrusion.

"Sorry, I didn't know anyone had come in."

Embarrassed, Lori hurried back to her office. She sank heavily on the high-back leather desk chair.

First sight of Jared had rubbed her on-edge nerves raw. The new job would be far more stressful than she could've imagined it. She'd already embarrassed herself and only one word described her new boss: Gorgeous.

No way could she work for a man that handsome and keep the needed sense of propriety for the job. Instead of focusing on work, she'd walk around daydreaming about nights in his arms.

Jared and Chuck walked through the conference room into her office.

"Jared Bolton, this is Lori Manning, your AA." Charlie introduced them.

"Good morning, Lori. Nice name, it'll be easy to remember."

Jared locked her in his gaze. His dark grey eyes smiled down into hers. He took her right hand, clammy with perspiration, and gripped it in a firm, lingering shake. Lori felt certain he had signaled interest in more than a professional relationship.

She stuttered and blushed as if she had met a rock star. Yet, through it all, she couldn't help but wonder what it was about her that had sparked his quick interest. Surely, a man with that much appeal was married or had a gorgeous girlfriend. She noted but ignored the mental warning that he was fast on his feet with women.

From their first meeting, flirting and romantic tension stirred between them. Her every awake thought centered on Jared. He filled her nightly dreams. Within a few weeks, they'd started bumping into each other outside the office. At first, they showed up at the same spots accidentally on purpose. The company didn't prohibit employee fraternization, but of course, didn't encourage it either. Both kept it hidden but before long, they had become inseparable.

All her adult life she had wished a man like Jared would come along. He fit the perfect male image she had pictured: Long muscular legs, well developed upper body, always restless and on the move. His thick, dark, gray-flecked hair and his chiseled features, along with the expensive slacks and polo shirts he wore, gave him a dash of rugged outdoor sophistication. His eyes followed her around the office as if he enjoyed her constant presence.

Before long, Lori couldn't keep the romance a secret. She just had to share the news of her fabulous relationship. Beth was the person she wanted most to brag about it to.

Introducing Beth and Jared face-to-face never crossed her mind. She knew Beth was the last person on earth she could trust. After their last conflict, Lori had sworn if Beth lured away another one of her boyfriends, she would kill her. However, in spite of their past problems, Lori knew Beth was the one person who could keep a secret. They'd known each other all their lives. They had grown up on the same street and had been inseparable. Both had the same taste in things. When Lori got parakeets, Beth wanted parakeets as well, even though she had a cat. As teenagers, both complained to each other about their mothers. Until Beth moved to Pine Ridge, they both still lived at home with their parents.

Since Beth no longer worked at the same office, Lori felt safe discussing Jared with her. Long before he arrived at the company, Accounting had transferred Beth offsite. She now worked at a remote office in the woods near Pine Ridge. Jared never visited that location. Beth came to the Hamilton Mills office once or twice a year for mandatory company meetings.

Looking back, Lori wanted to kick herself for being so stupid. She'd shared the news without reservation.

"You've always grabbed the great looking guys first," she'd gloated during the phone conversation she'd initiated. "Absolutely dreamy . . . member of a wealthy Chicago family . . . single . . . drives an expensive sports car . . . long distance runner . . . college football captain. He's definitely the one." At the time, she didn't know Beth had won her two-year battle to move back to head office. Nor, did Beth tell her.

"Hey there, Lori."

Two days later Lori looked up from invoices stacked on her desk. Beth Hines stood before her grinning. At first glance, Lori knew that Beth was out to attract someone. Instead of the jeans and tee shirts she wore working with the lumberjacks, she had on a low-cut red and white silk print blouse teamed with a stunning silk navy blue pants suit.

"You never visit when you come here," Lori noted.

28

"What gives?"

"I've moved back to Accounting. Came by to get a peek at your new boyfriend," Beth smirked. "The way you raved about him I can't wait to meet him."

Lori fell ill.

Struck with an instant devastating condition her hands started to tremble. Her palms broke out in sweat. Perspiration beaded on her face. Her churning stomach threatened to make her hurl. High school was happening all over again. Beth couldn't have made her intentions any clearer if she'd put them into words.

Aware that she had to discourage Beth's visit, Lori tried to keep Beth and Jared apart until Lori had the chance to warn him about Beth, "H-he's in a-a meeting . . . Will b-be there all afternoon," stuttering Lori watched the conference room door.

Beth hung around making small talk:

'Stuck in the middle of forest hell . . . finally, back to civilization . . . Hated the cramped trailer . . . Uncivilized loggers . . . tobacco spitting tree monkeys . . .'

Beth left then returned an hour later.

"He's still busy," Lori advised.

At that moment, as if she had summoned him, Jared opened the conference room door and stepped into her office for a peek at his messages.

Lori stood, "Jared, may I speak—"

"Well aren't you the handsome one," Beth interrupted, "Lori said you were good-looking, but she failed to mention 'drop dead dreamy'. I'm Beth Hines. I work in Accounting." Hand extended, eyes locked on his, she walked toward Jared, hips swaying, brazenly flirting.

Lori never had an opportunity to pull him aside.

Jared just stood there captivated, as if his eyes couldn't believe the creature before them existed.

Beth's lustrous dark curls framed her face. Her violet eyes peeked through a wilderness of lashes—

Footsteps now racing behind her at once brought Lori

back to the present.

"Lori, wait."

At the sound of Jared's voice, she turned around and watched him run from the garage toward her.

"Grab your bag and follow us out. Old Mill Road is too dangerous for a woman alone. If something happens, I'll never forgive myself."

"Thanks, Jared, but it's still early. Once everyone leaves, I'll tail Sheriff Tate out."

"You did a good job, Lori, setting up the picnic . . ." Jared's dark eyes lit with appreciation, "Your hard work didn't go unnoticed. Several supervisors complimented you as well. Maybe it's time for a raise—"

"Jared, we have to go, now," Beth ran back, took his arm, drew him away mid-sentence.

Lori strolled inside even more pleased with the way the picnic had turned out. She boarded the waiting elevator hoping Jared would follow through with the raise. She could use it. For a long time she had been wanting a new car. A raise would help her swing it.

The image of a little blue sports car held behind her sights, Lori unlocked the office door. She glanced outside the window just as Jared and Beth made their way toward Old Mill Road. Afraid the sudden light might draw their attention to her watching from the window Lori left them off and stood in the dimness as Jared and Beth left the complex.

Jared was in the lead. The waning sunlight glinted off the hood of his Apple Red Lamborghini.

Her gaze followed the car: When she and Jared dated, she'd felt like she owned it.

Jared split the week between Hamilton Mills and Quail Valley. When work demanded all his time, he would ask her to have the car serviced.

As she sat behind the wheel on butter-soft leather seats, top down, wearing designer sunglasses, she felt like a movie star as she sped off for Pine Ridge or the service station north of town to avoid having a hassle with Jimmy Jay.

Loggers and farmers whistled and honked as she sped past them on the road.

Although the personal car service wasn't a part of her office duties, Lori took over the upkeep so Jared would have one less worry. When he and Beth started dating, Lori gave Beth the keys and the upkeep responsibility. But Beth's supervisor wouldn't let her do it on company time.

Now, Jared forgot to fuel the car. He often had Jimmy bring gas to the office so he wouldn't run out on the road.

'Not ready for a serious relationship . . .'

Long after Jared and Beth had gone, Lori stared out the window unaware that the room grew dark along with the fading outside light. Her thoughts had traveled back to a Friday night soon after Jared met Beth.

The night he broke up with Lori.

At the Watering Hole in Pine Ridge, an expensive bottle of red wine on the table. Jared quietly worked on a third glass. It was obvious he had something on his mind. Earlier they'd made small talk. Since then they'd sat in silence. Finally:

"Maybe we should think about seeing other people," Jared said.

Surprised hurt almost choked her.

Lori plastered the over-sized wine goblet to her lips, drained the contents. Her hands shook as she poured more wine. Thank goodness, the two glasses she'd already drunk had relaxed her a little. Otherwise, she would've made a complete fool of herself.

While she fought back tears, a panicking inner voice said she couldn't let him go. She'd never find another man like Jared. He fulfilled her every fantasy. She should beg him not to end the relationship. Then anger filled her thoughts. He was breaking up with her so he could see Beth. She should throw wine in his face. Again, tears threatened. She downed a fourth then a fifth glass of wine.

Refusing to reveal how much his suggestion had upset her, Lori silently vowed to make Beth pay for what she had done. After the mood swings had settled, Lori forced a smile as she explained her long silence: "I've always heard that great minds run in the same channels." She shook her head in disbelief. "It has crossed my mind a few times that we should slow things down a bit. However, I wasn't sure how to approach it. Since you feel the same way, I think we should consider it."

Apparently, Jared had expected a different reaction. Her response seemed to catch him off-guard. He showed a side of himself she had never witnessed. His face flamed as he leapt to his feet then hurried from the table. As he strode for the men's room, he impatiently signaled the waiter for more wine.

Right then Lori knew Jared couldn't handle being on the receiving end of rejection. He could give it, but he couldn't take it. When he returned, his eyes remained dark but he added a disclaimer, "It needn't be a done deal. We'll try it for a while. If we see it's not working, we can always get back together."

Now, footsteps leading down the hall in her direction penetrated her thoughts. Brought back to the present, Lori flipped on the light switch.

Fluorescence flooded the room as Sheriff Tate stepped through the door. Tate had traded his sheriff's hat for a Hamilton Mills logo cap. He'd teamed black western boots with his blue-gray uniform.

An odd, distant man in his fifties, whenever Tate engaged in a conversation, he avoided making eye contact. His gaze always rested off in the distance. 'The eyes are the windows to the soul' Lori's mother often said. Her mother believed Tate had something hidden in his past he feared his eyes would reveal.

Tate owned a horse ranch just outside of town. Thin and rangy, he looked more suited to riding a horse than driving the beat up cruiser. On his days off, he rode Old

Mill Road alone on horseback late into the night.

Rumors said he planned to run for mayor in the next election.

"Ready, Lori?" Tate asked.

She checked her watch, "I can't leave while we still have visitors."

"Jimmy Jay's waiting at the garage to take a look at the cruiser to see why it keeps cutting out. May need to leave it there overnight . . ." Tate's voice trailed off as he gazed at the forest, "Can't get parts till tomorrow. I'll have Buzz pick me up."

"Deputy Weston's still around? I thought he had long gone." She wasn't all that fond of Buzz but pretended an interest just to make conversation. Tall and good-looking, Buzz dated women until he got bored then tossed them aside like broken dolls. Whenever he and Lori came in contact, he tried to devise ways to get them together.

"Rounding up everybody before he heads out. Before he takes off, he'll see if you're ready to leave," Tate headed for the door.

"Thanks, leftovers in the fridge if you want any," Lori yelled thinking Tate was halfway down the hall.

His head popped back through the opening, "Wouldn't mind fixing a plate for later then I'll send the stragglers home. The Johnsons are chasing down their kids. I'll ask them to let you know when they're ready in case Buzz leaves while they're still here."

Lori gathered the sales invoices on her desk then took them to the file cabinets.

Locked . . .

Annoyed that she'd forgotten she'd locked the cabinets Lori strode back to the desk, opened a drawer, snatched out her purse. She located the keys on the bottom of the bag beneath Beth's and her cell phones. All of which reminded her to leave Beth's phone on the credenza in Accounting when Lori passed there headed to the lunchroom. On Monday, someone would discover it and think Beth laid it there then walked off without it.

Lori filed the invoices; relocked the cabinet. She pocketed the keys then grabbed a storage box full of old file folders and dropped it on the conference room table.

While she straightened the office, she recalled having lunch with Anne Johnson last Tuesday at the Fireside Lodge. The popular log cabin inn and restaurant three miles from the office nestled off the road beneath towering pines. Inside the restaurant, mounted above two stone fireplaces deer, moose, bear, and boar heads kept watch over the room. Decorated to appeal to the hunters and sportsmen who frequented the inn, walleye fish, wading boots, rods, reels, tackle, and hunting gear wandered the dining area.

She and Anne had slipped into a booth, ordered seafood salads, and then checked the walls for the latest additions. The owner always brought back trophies from his frequent hunting trips.

"How's your day going?" Anne had asked.

"So-so," Lori shrugged.

Anne had worked at Hamilton Mills since her high school graduation. A petite blonde five years older than Lori, Anne had four kids and an attorney husband she adored. Their conversation first centered on the job, the gorgeous summer weather, and town gossip. Soon, as all conversations inevitably did, the talk turned to the murders.

"Lori, I'm not sure I believe Jimmy Jay's the killer. I know everybody else thinks he is, but what about Buzz-What's His-Face? He seems a little too smooth. His parents moved away while he was in high school. He's been back in Pine Ridge—what—three years? Nobody knows what went on in his life while he was gone. He patrols alone at night . . ." Anne paused. Looking thoughtful: "So does the sheriff and we all know what a strange duck he is."

"Karl Weston," Lori provided Buzz's name as she

pushed her water glass aside, making room for the waiter to serve her salad and lemonade.

"Why do they call him Buzz? Every time those two Mellencamp guys come around they start ribbing him about it," Anne noted.

"It's short for Buzzard and definitely not a story you want to hear while you're eating."

"I have kids, remember. There's little I haven't heard at the dinner table."

"Knock, knock . . ."

Lori jumped and looked up. She'd been lost so deep in thought she hadn't heard the elevator doors open. Buzz now filled the doorway.

"Good grief, Buzz you startled me."

"Your mind was lost way out there somewhere. Must've been thinking about your boyfriend."

"Yeah, right . . ."

"I'm heading out, ready to go?"

"I still have things to do here. Don't wait. I'll leave when the Johnsons do."

"Doing anything special tonight?"

"Going home and relax. It's been a long day."

"The evening's still young. If you change your mind, some of us are getting together at the Green Cypress. Drop by. I'll save you a seat and buy you a drink." Buzz tossed a careless wave goodbye then strode for the elevator.

Not in a million years, Lori stood thinking. If she met Buzz at the Green Cypress tonight, tomorrow it would be rumored all over town that they were an item. Besides, she couldn't let her hair down and drink as much as she wanted to. It would be just her luck her dad would meet his beer pals there tonight.

Lori again looked outside. The Sturgeon Moon angled up the pines. The sight of it brought back something she'd learned in school about the old fishing Indians. They'd named the August full moon a 'Sturgeon Moon' because the fish were always more plentiful during that time.

Now as she continued straightening the office, she recalled seeing Jimmy Jay earlier today standing in the food line.

Her combining thoughts traveled back to the conversation she had with Anne last Tuesday about Jimmy and about how Buzz got his name. A frown creased her brow. Buzz hadn't changed all that much since high school. She could see him involved in something just as dumb now.

"Buzz, Tony, and Ralph were in tenth grade," she'd told Anne last Tuesday at lunch. "They went bird hunting near the area where the murders happen now. Buzz spotted a turkey buzzard's nest on a utility pole then decided to climb up and take an egg from it. When he reached the nest, the female was on it. He shoved his hand under her and she puked all over him. He stunk so awful Tony and Ralph wouldn't let him near them. His mother made him strip outside and bathe in cold water from the hose. Tony and Ralph started calling him 'Buzzard Puke'. Now it's just Buzz."

"Buzzard puke, eeew! Can you imagine having that all over you?" Anne laughed, shuddered, and made a face all at the same time. "Will I be cool or what when I gross out my kids at dinner. They'll love it although Greg might not think it's funny. Now all that silliness between those guys makes sense."

"I'd bet a year's salary Jimmy Jay's the killer," Lori revisited Anne's earlier comment about him. "Remember all the trouble he's gotten into over the years?"

"I heard about the bullying. I'd graduated when you guys reached high school, but word got around. Back then, he sang in the church choir. Even at that age, he had the most beautiful baritone voice I've ever heard. He always looked so sad. I suspected it was because of the fighting. Later, I heard he'd started breaking faces. Once he quit school, he stopped coming to church."

"He became the bully. Got drunk, picked fights, disrespected women . . . Everybody said he'd kill someone sooner or later."

"I feel sorry for him . . . growing up without his mother, no friends. He doesn't know how to respect women. Repairing cars with his dad and grandpa and listening to his mother's old classical music was all he knew. Since his dad and grandpa died, he has no one left."

Lori forked a chunk of Dungeness crabmeat from her salad. "He eats like a pig. It's obvious he's never been house broken."

"Is he still sweet on you?" Anne teased.

"Since third grade," Lori gritted recalling how Jimmy use to stare at her in class then at recess corner her on the playground asking for a kiss. "Even then I couldn't stand him," she told Anne. "I'd already decided I would marry someone rich and handsome when I grew up. This salad is the best, ever."

"Look at all the crabmeat," Anne agreed. "Jimmy's not bad looking, just overweight and needs to lose the beard. Speaking of marriage, has anyone said why Mildred and Tate split up?"

"Probably because he's half nuts. Thinks he's the Headless Horseman . . . rides alone at night through the woods—"

"Hides behind the bushes on Main Street hoping to catch someone run the one traffic light that never works," added Anne.

Both fell into giggles.

"I heard . . . he plans to run for . . . mayor," Anne had trouble controlling her laughter.

"That should be interesting." Lori sat back and shook her head, grinning.

Anne leaned forward and lowered her voice, "Time for another murder, been almost six months since the last one."

She shuddered:

"This picnic thing gives me the willies. The whole town'll be there. There'll be a lot of beer drinking. Some guy will get drunk; pick a fight with his wife, or girlfriend, or both and she'll huff off by herself then wind up dead. Our next-door neighbor told Greg he saw Buzz parked on Old Mill Road the night of the last murder. A woman on the back seat of the cruiser looked like she'd been crying. Buzz was supposed to be patrolling the hill area that night."

"Sounds like one of those tales that crop up after every murder. He and Tate will cover the picnic grounds together. They'll make sure no one leaves alone. There won't be any trouble," Lori assured her.

Lori now gathered her thoughts. Her awareness back to the present she again looked out the window. Soon it would be dark. The last slivers of sunlight slowly faded behind the pines. Along this stretch of road on into Pine Ridge, federal and state protected century old forest pines reached from the ravines and touched the sky.

At nightfall, the forest turned pitch black. With each passing breeze, fingers of moonlight poked through the dense growth and chased darting shadows across the road.

Beth Hine's coming encounter with Jimmy rushed to mind: She'll be terrified.

I know her well thought Lori. Beth hadn't spoken to Jimmy since high school because she believed he spread the rumor she slept with him in exchange for her car repairs. However, to save her butt now Beth would screw Jimmy's brain out and swear she wouldn't breathe a word about it.

Unaware that she did so, Lori absently brushed her fingers up and down her throat. Beth had never once suspected that Lori had started the rumor. *Lori took my Popsicle.* Her thoughts suddenly traveled back to Beth outside on the porch swing slurping the ill-gained Popsicle and cleverly smirking. That lie began her resentment of Beth, Lori recalled. In addition, she had never forgiven her mother for letting Beth's claim go unchallenged.

A few weeks after Beth took the Popsicle tears washed the smirk off her face. She and her family were in Pine Ridge having dinner when Lori snuck into their house through an unlocked window. She placed Beth's parakeets on the floor then called in the cat. From her perch on Beth's bed, Lori smiled as she watched Prissy pounce on the birds.

One parakeet flew from the room then out the open window.

Lori trudged home disappointed that Prissy had killed only one bird. Later, Beth thought Prissy had eaten both birds and blamed her mother for leaving the cage door open.

Nightfall can't come soon enough Lori now muttered. She wanted Beth over and done with. Her lying, man grabbing, and arrogance had gotten old. If for no other reason, she should die for the bitchy remark she'd made earlier: 'You've been gone so long I thought you were out hunting a new boyfriend.'

All of a sudden fuming, Lori grabbed both cell phones then dashed for the elevator. She should've answered Beth's comment with, 'Why? Are you waiting to claim another one of my castoffs?' That, however, would've started a war of words between Lori and Jared. She wanted him to go on believing she harbored no ill feelings over the breakup. Later, she would make him pay for what he'd done.

She rode the elevator down hoping nothing ever came up that would implicate her in the murder.

Lori remembered to make sure both hers and Beth's cell phones were on. If somebody called her number asking about Beth, she'd reply, 'Beth's not here. I have no idea why she doesn't answer her phone.'

As soon as the elevators doors opened on the first floor, Lori strode through them. She followed the hall winding through a menagerie of Northwest wilderness animals captured on the wall hangings. Soaring eagles, majestic moose, bighorn sheep balanced precariously on mountainsides, snarling black bears, all watched her unlock the accounting office door.

Cracking the door open only wide enough to slip her hand inside and place Beth's phone on the credenza, Lori then pulled the door shut and jerked the key from the lock all in the same motion. She continued around the hall, headed for the break room shoving the key ring in her pocket as she went. If she ever had to explain why her fingerprints were on Beth's phone, she would pause and think back carefully. She would then explain that Beth had dropped it earlier, Lori picked it up, and then handed it back to Beth.

As she passed the main copy room, through the open door Lori noticed that someone had opened a new carton of paper. A ream had been taken out, opened, a handful of paper removed, and the remainder left in the open package on the table.

Her temper flared.

She rushed into the room, grabbed the paper from the package, opened the nearest copy machine drawer, and then shoved the paper into it. Her right foot slammed the drawer shut, 'Why in hell's name can't these damned people ever fill the paper tray? Putting a few sheets in it takes just as much time and effort as adding the whole damned ream.' Still fuming, as she turned to go, she grabbed the box top also left on the table. She reached to place it back on the carton then suddenly realized she needed it to hold the leftovers she planned to take home. She held onto it then stormed for the kitchen.

In the spacious employee lunchroom, dining sets, two large refrigerators, vending machines, TVs, and couches made up the furnishings. Lori laid her phone on top of the refrigerator containing the picnic leftovers. If the phone rang while she filled her plates, she wouldn't need to reach in her pocket for it. She then grabbed a handful of take-out boxes from the stack she'd placed on the refrigerator during the cleanup earlier.

Fifteen miles stretched between the office and Highway 209, she heaped smoked ham and brisket on a plate thinking. Beth and Jared would reach the intersection at dusk. When Jared turned back, it would be dark. Soon afterward Beth would run out of gas.

Fear of becoming a murder victim had made Beth paranoid. The murders dominated her conversations. Investigation had found that each woman had contacted a family member as soon as her car stopped running. However, when help arrived, she was nowhere around. The next day searchers discovered her body halfway down the gorge.

Beth always said that if she ever ran out of gas, or if she had car trouble on the road, she wouldn't stick around. As she called for help, she would run from the area as fast as she could and keep whoever answered the phone on the line until help showed up.

Tonight, while she fled for her life, the big black tow truck would creep up behind her—

"Lori," Sheriff Tate appeared in the doorway. "The Johnsons are the only visitors left. They'll let you know when they're ready to go. Jimmy's at the garage waiting. You can leave when the Johnson's do."

"Great," answered Lori surprised that Tate was still there. His continued presence again reminded her of the dangers the area posed. Tate's mention of Jimmy Jay also brought back memory of her run-in with Jimmy soon after his release from the state mental hospital.

The court had ordered him to undergo psychiatric evaluation at the Pine Ridge Mental Institution after he punched Councilman Cecil Jones' lights out. Cecil had refused to approve some tow charges because Jimmy had damaged two county vehicles he'd towed. Jimmy's answer was a right jab that broke Cecil's nose.

Both incidents happened just before the murders

started. Her fight with Jimmy came on her way home from visiting her parents after their move to Pine Ridge.

It was a perfect springtime Sunday evening just before sunset. Lori drove with the windows open. The scent of wild strawberries and blackberry blossoms perfumed the air. She had reached the crossroads and braked at the stop sign when her right front tire started hissing.

Her heart sank.

The tire was losing air. At first, she couldn't imagine why. Recently, she had put all new tires on the car. Something on the road must've—

Jimmy Jay.

Several people around town had complained about having flat tires in that area. They suspected Jimmy scattered tacks on Old Mill Road to drum up business.

She wouldn't pay him a red cent to change the tire, Lori decided. She'd do it herself. Moments later, she stood in front of the car staring helplessly at the tire. She had no idea where to begin. Soon, she had to renege on her decision. She'd never changed a tire before in her life. If she ran into trouble and couldn't finish it before dark . . .

Angry and near tears knowing how much the tire had cost, and thinking about the unnecessary delay the flat had caused, she limped on it through the intersection to Cooper's garage.

Jimmy stood outside, his head under the hood of a county pickup truck. Bexar County contracted him to keep their vehicles running.

Without question, Jimmy was the best mechanic around. People called him names, but everyone agreed that when it came to vehicle repair no other mechanic in the county matched him.

An Italian opera blared from the garage radio. Jimmy didn't hear her car rumble up.

Lori pulled in close behind him then laid on the horn.

Jimmy jumped, banged his head on the hood.

It should've broken your stupid neck, Lori thought

hoping something horrible happened to him.

His blue overalls covered in grease, Jimmy lumbered to her door wadding an oily shop towel between his meaty palms, cursing. When he recognized her, he started grinning.

"You shouldn't of drove on that tire, Lori." He leaned against the car door. His piercing blue eyes impaled her through the open window. "You could've ruined a brand new tire."

She didn't even bother to explain that she'd just picked up something near the intersection. Her icy stare answered for her.

Jimmy jerked a thumb toward an empty service bay.

Lori remained inside the car while he lifted it on the rack.

"How much?" She asked once he'd finished.

"For you a kiss," Jimmy eyed her lips.

She deliberately looked him over. Her gaze roamed his greasy cover-ups, heaving belly, unruly red hair creeping from beneath a dirty John Deere logo cap, breadcrumbs littering his beard.

"Jimmy Jay, you're a pig. I'd rather die first."

"I'll show you my pig," he grabbed the door—

Just then, Sheriff Tate drove up.

Beginning the day the murders started happening, Tate and Bexar County Homicide Investigators had worked on the case. Jimmy was their lone suspect, but repeated questioning found no evidence against him. Jimmy knew the whole town thought he was the killer and enjoyed playing the villain. Any time he passed a former female classmate on the streets he crossed his eyes, leered insanely, and then slashed his left forefinger past his throat.

Just as she always did when she recalled the murders, Lori shuddered. She'd known all the dead women. They'd been classmates in high school. All had worked at Hamilton Mills and all had sworn they would never let

Jimmy breed.

Lori now placed the foil wrapped leftovers she'd packed for dinner inside the box top. Hunger rippled in her stomach. All day long the picnic had kept her so busy she hadn't sat down and enjoyed a full meal.

Carrying the box top, she boarded the elevator back to the third floor. Inside the office, she looked out at the forest now silhouetted in shadows. The Johnsons had parked inside the garage on the first floor and were loading their lawn chairs in the trunk.

Soon, Beth would run out of gas.

The sound of the elevator doors captured Lori's attention. Moments later, giggling voices and running footsteps echoed in the hall.

"We're ready," Mindy and Becca, Anne's eight and ten year-old tousled haired daughters appeared in the doorway, "We've parked near your car in the garage so you won't be back there alone."

"Thanks ladies," Lori grabbed her purse from the desk drawer.

Right then the phone on her desk started ringing. Lori checked the caller ID.

Jared Bolton . . . Why is he calling here?
Probably looking for Beth. Don't answer it.
Answer, it might come in handy later.
"Hamilton Mills . . ."

"Lori, you're still there?" Surprise filled Jared's voice. "I've been calling around trying to reach someone."

"Just leaving."

Mouthing to Mindy and Becca: "Tell Anne I'm on the way."

"Have you spoken with Beth?" Jared asked.

"No. Why?" Lori bristled.

"She doesn't answer her phone."

(No comment)

"I've run out of gas. Forgot to tank up this morning. I had just turned back for town when I ran out. I'm a mile or so past the Crossroads on Old Mill Road, parked in the Lovers Leap area. Can you swing by and give me a lift home? Jimmy Jay's working on Tate's cruiser. My call transferred to County Dispatch. They'll tell Jimmy to bring gas and pick me up at home tomorrow morning so I can drive to the race."

Lori dashed for the garage, apologized to the Johnsons for the delay, and then tailed them from the complex.

Amazed at the speed in which the heavy heartedness she'd lived with for months had lifted and how fast happiness had replaced it, she started singing an old Ray Charles tune: *Together Again . . .*

Soon Jared and she would be back together. After she drove him home, he would likely invite her in for a drink. They'd talk:

She would say she was happy for him and Beth; they made a great looking couple.

(Yeah, right)

Knowing Beth would soon be out of the picture, she could afford to be generous.

Twenty minutes later, Lori and the Johnsons reached the Crossroads. The Johnsons braked at the stop sign then turned left onto Highway 209 where Lori would've turned had she been headed straight home. Instead, she continued through the intersection and remained on Old Mill Road. Across the street to her right set Cooper's garage.

The service station's lights were on, but she saw no sign of the tow truck. Sheriff Tate's cruiser stood before a closed service bay door. However, he was nowhere in sight. Apparently, as he'd suspected, the cruiser needed a part Jimmy Jay didn't have stocked. Jimmy had driven Tate home or Buzz had picked him up when he passed through there earlier.

Either way, Lori swallowed uneasily; Jimmy Jay was on the prowl. He could be killing Beth right now.

Her heart skipped a beat.

Her foot involuntarily mashed the accelerator.

As the speedometer climbed, the yellow headlight beams raced through the dark ahead like spools of unwinding ribbon.

Deer Crossing . . .

A buck pictured on a road sign reminded Lori to stay alert for them. She lightened the pressure on the gas pedal. Deer were unpredictable. Any moment, one startled by something could leap onto the road. Skunks and other small animals were also on the move. Her dad once hit a skunk and the musk reeked on his truck for weeks.

No one passed her headed in either direction as she drove. Since the murders started happening, few people traveled the road at night.

At night Old Mill Road's deserted. The chills of death fill the air . . .

A blizzard of moths fell before the headlights. Badgers and raccoons' eyes glowed alongside the road.

As she watched the pavement now starting to curve, Lori recalled the many nights she and Jared had traveled Old Mill Road when they dated. Every weekend that he didn't work or run, they drove to Pine Ridge. Unlike the ten thousand residents that made up Pine Hollow's population, Pine Ridge boasted close to a hundred thousand people. Many places to eat and drink, they both loved Mexican. Warm evenings like this found them winding Dead Man's Curve, convertible top down, wind blowing their hair, both laughing at something silly they'd seen or overheard.

Her eyes misted. Some nights on the drive home, they'd park at Lovers Leap and make out under the stars.

They were so good together she had thought the romance would never end.

Soon, it will be like old times again.

Lori eased off the accelerator and let her speed drop to thirty. She entered Dead Man's Curve and followed it effortlessly. A black wall of pines rose on each side of the road. Overhead, stars flowered brightly on the black prairie sky. The curve saw more than its share of fatal accidents she drove thinking. Drivers ignored the speed limit posted on the reflective railings then sped into the surprisingly sharp turn. They lost control and entered oncoming traffic, which resulted in head-on collisions. Or, they over-corrected and plunged down the gorge.

Starting to worry, Lori completed the curve. She checked the odometer. She had traveled farther than she'd expected to. She thought Jared had said he was located near the Lovers Leap area. If she drove much farther, she could come up on Beth stranded—

Flashing emergency lights—

Lori hit the brakes.

She stopped the car hard then sat spotlighted in the high beams of a huge, black vehicle blocking both lanes of the road.

The seconds ticked by while she digested the scene before her. Jimmy Jay was about to tow Jared's car. He had aligned the wrecker's rear end with the front end of the Lamborghini.

What's he doing here?

Jared had said Jimmy would drive him to the car tomorrow morning.

Jimmy lumbered from behind the truck checking his cell phone. Her eyes strained through the headlight glare for a glimpse of Jared sitting inside the truck.

Jimmy dimmed the headlights but left the emergency lights flashing. "Hunting for a date, Lori?" He ambled toward her snickering.

"I'm here to pick up Jared and drive him home." She ignored Jimmy's asinine remark. If she didn't know better, she would swear he had been talking with Beth. Earlier, she'd made a similar crappy comment.

"Gone home."

"Gone home? How's he getting home?" Her voice shrilled.

"Called Dispatch; said a logger came along and offered

him a ride. He left word for me to bring gas for the car when I pick him up tomorrow morning so he can run in the race. Since it wasn't too far out of the way, I thought I'd come out and tow it to the station so it won't be left on the road—"

"He must've gotten a ride as soon as he hung up." Lori interrupted.

"Why'd he have you come out here for him? If he'd waited a little longer, I could've brought him some gas."

Lori detected criticism in Jimmy's tone, "If it's any of your business, he's my supervisor."

"Miss Smarty Pants, have you checked your phone? Maybe Jared left a message for you to go home."

Lori dug in her cargo pockets for the phone. She then grabbed her purse and began a search inside it. "No! No! No!" Growing more frantic by the moment, she kept looking, realizing even as she did so she had left her phone on top of the refrigerator at work. Now she knew why Jared had called her on the office phone. He couldn't reach her on the cell.

Jimmy Jay stood at the door. Hands shoved inside his pockets, he leered through the open window. "Get out, Lori; let me show you that piggy you're always talking about."

Panic, fear, nausea—all twisted inside her at once. Sudden realization struck her: Jared was gone; she and Jimmy Jay were there alone.

Get out of here, fast. Not forward, the tow truck's blocking the road.

Lori whipped the car around in a dizzying U-turn, floored the accelerator. The tires screeched and threw gravel as the car lurched—

An explosion—then another rocked the night.

Dear God Jimmy's firing.

Screaming, she fought to control the car.

"You okay?" Jimmy ran to the front passenger door, "Two blow-outs. You picked up some nails."

Unsure what exactly had happened, Lori lay huddled against the door. Jimmy stared inside as he summed up the situation. Then a laugh rumbled from his throat. He threw back his head, opened his mouth, and released a long howl. He grabbed the door handle, "It's just you and the Big Bad Wolf now—"

"Jimmy Jay," Lori vaguely heard County Dispatcher Jack Rhodes' voice crackle from the tow truck radio, "Cypress and Canyon Road; clear a two-car pile-up."

Jimmy turned on a run for the truck. Over his shoulder: "C'mon, Lori, I'll give you a lift home, fix your tires tomorrow."

Lori remained inside the car. Through the rearview mirror, she saw Jimmy unhitch Jared's car, snap a cell phone picture of the front end, jump inside the truck, and then nose the hood even with the front of her sedan.

He looked down at her through the windshield. "Suit yourself," he yelled from his lowered window, "You'll be here when I get back. Nobody's coming along and you ain't got your phone." His next words hung in the air for emphasis. "After I feel you up . . ." He turned on the cabin light so she could see him slash his left forefinger past his throat.

Moments later, the taillights disappeared around the curve.

Collapsing into sobs, Lori slumped over the steering wheel. Terrifying thoughts filled her head: She had been there alone with Jimmy Jay. Jared—no one knew she'd come across him. She'd never seen Jimmy more menacing. His eyes had burned into her like hot coals. Had Dispatch not called by now she would be dead.

Tomorrow, Jared's car would still be there and no one would know Jimmy had come to tow it. County Dispatch could only say they had given him the information. They'd later called Jimmy to clear an accident but didn't know his whereabouts at the time.

Don't think about that now Lori told herself. Reaching

home before Jimmy comes back is the bigger problem. Once he clears the wreckage, he'll return.

As soon as her weakened legs would carry her, she would start running as fast as she could. At the same time, she would keep an eye out for Jimmy sneaking up on her in the dark.

Her eyes probed the forbidding night. The mere thought of leaving the car then walking alone almost five miles home terrified her. She'd grown up hearing tales about prison escapees hidden out in the woods, bears, Bigfoot . . . UFOs hovered above the treetops . . .

No matter how scary, she had to do it.

Lori inhaled a deep breath then held it while she summoned her courage. She kept a close watch on the blackness around her. The frogs and crickets that had quieted while Jimmy was there, had once again tuned a concerto alongside the road. She glanced back at Jared's car all but lost in the dark. She wished she'd made a set of the car keys before she'd given them to Beth. Had she done so, she could siphon her gas into his tank then drive herself home.

Lori released the uneasy hold she held on her breath then reached for her shoulder bag on the passenger seat beside her.

Why, Lori wondered, would Jimmy try to coax her from the car? He could've used the tools he carried that unlocked car doors if he'd wanted to kill her. Had he wanted to, he could've opened the door, dragged her out, and murdered her right there. Maybe she should've accepted his offer. After Dispatch called, he was in a hurry. He knew a sheriff's deputy waited at the accident scene. He wouldn't have driven her into town and let people see them together if he planned to kill her later. Likely, he would've taken her home and then hurried off to clear the accident. He would've waited for another opportunity to find her alone.

Somebody please come along . . .

Lori suddenly remembered that her dad sometimes drove to Pine Hollow and had a few beers at the Green Cypress Inn.

God, please let this be one of those nights.

CHAPTER EIGHT

Jimmy Jay lifted his foot off the accelerator; let the truck slow to a crawl.

Time had come to teach Lori a lesson. He watched the road ahead, thinking. Her nasty attitude had gotten on his nerves. All he'd ever done was rib her a little. She was an only child so he hadn't beat up her brothers in high school. She had no reason to be hostile. He should really piss her off; give her a reason to be mad. He should go back, take a kiss, and then demand that she apologize for calling him fat.

No matter how nice he treated her, she always cut him down. None of the women he'd attended school with ever acknowledged his presence without sarcasm. Anne Johnson was the one woman in town who always treated him nice.

Jimmy checked the dashboard clock. The tow job could wait. The accident would still be there whenever he showed up. They couldn't get it towed away any faster if they called a service in Pine Ridge. He had the only tow truck within forty miles.

Besides, he'd traveled only a mile or so away. In a few minutes, he could go back and teach Lori a lesson. If she still refused the ride, he'd give her his phone so she could have someone pick her up. She could drop the phone off at the station tomorrow. Jimmy mashed the brakes, whipped the truck around.

As he drove, he lowered both windows and let the night air fill his lungs. Ahead, under the truck lights, the silhouetted pines stood tall like giant sentries guarding both sides of the road. Upon his approach, they joined forces then rushed toward him *en masse*.

Seconds later, Jimmy lowered the volume on the Mozart CD then turned off the truck lights.

Seeing him come back might spook Lori. Likely, she had already started walking. She would take off running and screaming when he drove up. He'd have to chase her down. Catching her and letting her wiggle around in his arms would be fun, but he needed to clear the wreck before it caused another accident.

Jimmy had no problem driving without the headlights. He knew the area as well as he knew the backs of his hands. He knew the way the wind whipped through the pines and let the moonlight in, where the shadows settled deepest, the spots where he pulled off the road and parked completely hidden.

At night, wild creatures roamed the woods: deer, elk, bear, Bobcats. However, the two-legged animals acted the nuttiest. Before the murders started, lovers from around the county came and parked along Old Mill Road. Date rapes and assaults were common. Buzz arrested Tammie and Judith the town hookers then brought them out here. They had sex with him to keep out of jail.

Some people believed Lovers Leap held magic. Jimmy believed it too. If he ever found someone to marry, he would propose and get married right there the way some other people did. They believed the magic would keep them together. As legend had it, Lovers Leap got its name after a young Indian chief and an Indian princess from warring tribes met and fell in love there. When the elders refused to let them marry, they leapt into the bottomless pool to spend eternity together. Folks claimed they saw them on rainy nights holding hands above the Leap.

Dispatch had reported Jared's car out of gas there.

Sheriff Tate rode his horse, Shank, out here at night. Sometimes Tate took off all his clothes then rode Shank down the steep embankment. Not long ago, something down there spooked Shank. He crashed back up the gorge then high-tailed it down the road.

Jimmy had followed them in the dark laughing himself silly.

Shank wouldn't stop running until he reached home. Tate's wife drove in from playing bingo just as he galloped up buck-naked shouting 'Whoa'. A few days later, Mildred packed her clothes and left.

Jimmy now eased the truck off the road and drove alongside the canyon's edge, totally hidden within the dense roadside growth. He shut off the motor then stepped from the wrecker.

The earsplitting din of the frogs and crickets quieted.

The thick ground cover muffled his footsteps.

The night wrapped around him in silence. Anticipating the coming fun, Jimmy faded into the mist, grinning.

CHAPTER NINE

Lori shuddered.

All at once, the insects quieted. Cool air mingled with the warm.

The chills of death fill the air—

She jumped.

For a second, she thought she'd heard gravel crushing against the pavement. Unease rose inside her, goose bumps swelled on her arms. She listened hard. Likely deer, she soon decided.

Again, the crunching sounded . . . this time it drew nearer.

Something or someone hidden in the dark was walking toward her.

Her pulses pounded. Her eyes strained through the night. A shadow fell against the pavement.

Just a breeze moving the pines thought Lori—

Dear, Lord . . .

The shadow took shape: Big, broad . . .

Please . . . please . . . please Lori prayed, please don't let it be Jimmy Jay doubling back.

No, wait!

A quick thought cheered her. Maybe it's Beth. The

shadow didn't look like her, but shadows seldom resembled the images they reflected. Lori recalled the nights she left the gym and walked to her car. Her moon-cast shadow on the street looked nothing like her at all. The odd-shaped figure ahead could be Beth headed for Lori's car. She'd likely been in the area all along but had stayed out of sight while Jimmy Jay was there.

Lori watched the figure approach. Please, please be Beth, she begged. Beth had a set of Jared's keys. She often drove the car on the weekends that he worked. They would siphon gas from Lori's car into his. Or, if Beth didn't have the keys, they'd walk home together; lend each other moral support. Once they reached town, Beth could spend the night with her.

When this nightmare was ended, Lori vowed, she would stop fighting to win Jared back. Thank goodness only she knew what she'd planned for Beth earlier.

Had Jimmy murdered her then Jared and Lori reconciled, there'd always be another Beth. Jared was concerned only with himself. His and Beth's self-centered, narcissistic personalities left them no empathy for anyone else. The two deserved each other. In due time, they'd both destroy themselves.

As the figure drew closer, it grew more defined. Lori's hopes faded, too large and too tall for Beth. It looked more like Jimmy Jay.

Now, the car held her only hope for escape. Maybe she could drive it faster than he could run. Lori twisted the ignition; floored the accelerator. The car zigzagged and wobbled. The front tires ran off the rims and billowed smoke. The metal against the pavement shrieked and sparked as the car careened toward the gorge.

Wrestling the steering wheel, Lori aimed for the figure in the road.

He jumped clear, grabbed the back passenger door, and then ran along with the slow moving sedan.

A breeze swayed the pines. Moonlight mirrored off the

blade of a butcher knife he held in his hand. He wrenched the back door open then dove inside.

Insanely afraid, Lori threw her door open, jumped running and screaming from the moving vehicle.

Pounding footsteps soon raced up behind her.

The faster she ran, the footsteps drew nearer.

A hand reached out and grabbed her blouse. Strong arms pulled her back and locked around her. He wrestled her into the bushes, slammed her against the ground, and then dropped on top of her, pinning her down.

Lori stared into the enameled bowl of night sky. She recognized the star pattern above her head: The Big Dipper. Please, please let this be a nightmare her thoughts pleaded to it.

A sudden breeze parted the pines. Moonlight lifted the shadows off the attacker's face.

Although Lori knew the man pressing the knife against her throat, seeing him in this vicious animal-like state after he'd pretended to like her stunned her just the same. Her thoughts went on a wild search for words that might sway his intentions.

Offer him sex.

He's in control; he'll take whatever he wants, reminded a voice of reason.

Swear you won't report him if he lets you live . . .

Compassion and reasoning are not a part of his makeup. Your pleading is a part of the satisfaction he seeks. No matter what you say, he'll rape and then kill you, another thought opposed.

Without a word, Lori lost all hope. She lay in a daze ignoring his commands knowing nothing she did or didn't do would save her. The pleas of the other women he'd killed had fallen on deaf ears.

Silent tears slipped down her cheeks.

He took her willfully, without passion, sank his teeth deep into her lips; relished the taste of her blood. Lori recognized that he acted on some sick hidden need to punish her first.

A sudden slash of his left hand ignited a flame across her throat.

The fire blazed into her esophagus. Warmth gushed and spilled from the wound. Sounds of gurgling accompanied her labored breathing.

The Big Dipper faded.

Lori floated on a breeze above Dead Man's Curve; lingered briefly over the big black tow truck, heard drift from inside it the moody strains of Mozart's Fifth Symphony. A last look around committed the pine forest to the ages. Her final release of breath mingled with the forest breeze to ebb and flow there eternally.

CHAPTER TEN

Lori Manning is dead.

Tears flew down his cheeks.

Dazed, Jimmy eased back to the tow truck hearing only the rasp of his rapid breathing.

He wished with all his being that he could use it to breathe life back into her. Everything had happened so fast he never had the chance to tell her that he loved her. Or apologize for harassing her over the years. Or to say that he was sorry for the way things had turned out now.

His tears flowed unchecked.

After each murder, he had the same reaction; blinding tears, deep remorse; agonizing sorrow. From now on, Lori's death, along with the deaths of the other women would haunt him.

Her killing had sapped his strength like none of the others had; left him with just enough stamina to crawl back inside the truck. Since childhood, he'd had a crush on Lori although she'd despised him. He wished he could spend the night out here with her so she wouldn't be alone. But he couldn't chance someone coming along and discovering him.

Jimmy shook his head and then groaned.

When he went back to scare Lori, it never occurred to him that six months had passed since the last murder. Besides, not even for a minute had he ever imagined the sickness would claim her.

Earlier when he was here, he had failed to notice that it was the perfect spot for murder.

He'd come back only to scare her into apologizing.

However, like the times before he couldn't control the murder. It suddenly stepped in and took over.

Now, if somebody happened along, the authorities would arrest him for killing her. He couldn't pretend he knew nothing about it. This time faked ignorance wouldn't cut it. Even if he left unseen, his tire tracks so close to Lori's car proved he had been in the area around the time of her death. Circumstantial evidence alone would convict him just as public opinion had done in the other slayings.

Jimmy climbed inside the truck. His trembling right hand twisted the key in the ignition. Headlights off, he eased from the spot—

High beams—a fast approaching vehicle.

Jimmy stomped the brakes; the truck skidded sideways.

A speeding motorist rounded the curve. The car moved so fast the driver didn't see the tow truck nosing from the roadside growth.

Rooted to the spot Jimmy stared at the dashboard clock. His jaw muscles clenched, he heard only the sound of his warning thoughts:

Be careful on the drive back to town. The vehicle might park at Lovers Leap. When the tow truck passes, the driver will notice.

Go back to the murder scene.

No way.

You must.

Jimmy hated the very thought of going back but knew he would need proof when they asked him why he had been in the area.

When he felt certain the motorist had moved on, he

turned on the headlights then let the truck creep onto the road. He sped past Lori's car then maneuvered a quick turn on the narrow lanes. As he drove back, he recorded the scene on his cell phone.

Tomorrow, the investigators would discover the blood spattered weeds a short distance from Lori's car. Halfway down the canyon, they'd find her.

Jimmy killed the lights; let his eyes readjust to the dark, and then drove away. He kept a close watch on the distance ahead for approaching headlights. The rearview mirror reflected the blackness behind him.

Each of the dead women troubled his thoughts. He wondered why he couldn't simply view their deaths as payback for the way they'd treated him. But once they were dead so went his resentment. Now, he just wished he could bring them back.

Guided by the moonlight, Jimmy followed the dark curves. He longed for another road leading back to town. At the same time, he hoped the vehicle that had passed him earlier hadn't parked at Lovers Leap or at some other spot along the road.

As Jimmy neared the Leap, he shut off the motor then coasted in silence. Maybe anyone parked there would be too busy to notice him slip by.

Clear.

Only a lone ten-point buck, back dropped by the full moon, stood in the parking space above the Leap.

Jimmy released his breath. Until then he had been unaware that he held it. He grabbed the phone and captured an image of the magnificent moonlit creature.

A few minutes later, without further incident, he reached the Crossroads. Ignoring the stop sign, he crossed the intersection at an angle to the garage.

Leaving the motor running he stepped into the eerily still night. Only the thump of his boot heels against the pavement interrupted the quiet.

All this brought back to mind the long silent nights that

followed the deaths of his dad and grandfather. That frozen winter of grief that had stripped him to bare bones. Left him alone, a single maple naked and frozen among a forest full of firs. That same exposed feeling surrounded him now.

Jimmy hurried inside, turned off the lights. Earlier, he'd planned to come back and start work on Tate's cruiser so he had left them on. Now, he would be unable to concentrate. Once he cleared the accident, he would go straight home.

Jimmy rushed to the truck, jumped inside; activated the emergency lights. He then raced for the accident scene. As he neared it, he came to a decision: No more killings.

He would get help.

Too many women had died.

If he didn't seek help, in another six months the need to kill would rise again. Six months was the cooling off period between each slaying. Jimmy recognized the pattern and couldn't let it go on. He'd heard an FBI Criminal Profiler speak about the killings on TV. 'The Pine Hollow killer is an anger excitation rapist,' the Profiler had said. 'He gets his kicks from the victim's pleadings and seeing the pain on her face. He forces her to do things she doesn't want to do, but does them anyway to save her life. After she does what he says, he tells her no decent woman would do something like that. So, he kills her anyway,' the Profiler explained.

The Profiler had added that the killer had several reasons for raping and killing, but his main reason was to engage in sexual activity where he held complete control.

Jimmy wondered if lock-up and treatment would make recovery possible for that type of person.

Jimmy knew he couldn't go to the authorities alone; he needed someone he could trust to go with him. After the second murder, he had wanted to talk about the slayings, but feared if he confided in someone, it would turn out the way it did when his dad complained about the bullies.

Their parents ignored it, but the moment Jimmy defended himself the whole town made him the villain.

He wished he could trust Tate. However, Tate wanted to become the next mayor. He didn't stand a snowball's chance in hell right now, but if he arrested Jimmy, he'd be a shoo-in. Tate looked for ways to trap him. He dropped by the station at odd times pretending the cruiser needed work so he could snoop around. If Jimmy talked to Tate about the murders, Tate would railroad him and then profit from it.

'If you ever need anything . . .'

CHAPTER ELEVEN

"Lori Manning is dead.

"She was murdered. I was there."

The moment Greg and Anne Johnson opened the door the words spilled unguarded from his lips. While Jimmy had stood under the glare of the porch light waiting for an answer to his ring, he had recited what he would say. Growing more anxious by the moment, he'd soon lost his nerve and had turned to race for the truck when the door opened.

Now the heat from the porch light burned into his skull. Sweating and mumbling, details about the murders tumbled in disarray from his lips. "Tomorrow, when searchers find her, Tate will question me again. Everybody will say that I killed her. Nobody ever thinks about giving me the benefit of the doubt; that the situation might be out of my control. This time I want to tell Tate I have a lawyer and I don't have to answer any questions without my attorney present.

"I can pay whatever you want," his eyes locked on Greg's blank stare, "I once overheard a bank teller say I have more money deposited than anyone else in the county has. My dad and grandpa invested the service station's profits in the stock market. They left me more money than I'll ever spend. Added to what I earn on my own, your fee won't be a problem.

"I shouldn't have let the murders keep happening," Jimmy swallowed the sudden lump rising in his throat . . . Without warning, grief and sorrow overwhelmed him. He stopped talking then took a deep breath before he went on. "All along, I've wanted to end the killings, but I didn't know how to stop them.

"Today at the picnic while I waited in line I realized there was somebody I could talk to. You invited me back to church," he directed to Anne, "Said let you know if I ever needed anything. When I finished clearing a wreck, I came here to ask for someone's name at the County Seat I can trust."

Jimmy stopped short of saying that he knew Greg was a defense attorney with a partnership in Pine Ridge. He had hoped that when Greg heard the story, he would help him come up with a way to make them listen without prejudice when he went to the authorities.

If he went alone, they'd twist his words around and wouldn't listen to his explanation. After they threw him in jail, they'd charge him with first-degree murder. The whole town was so mad and scared there might be talk of stringing him up.

Anne and Greg just stood there staring into his face. Jimmy noted their set, cold expressions. He saw reflected in their eyes something that looked like hate. Right then he knew he'd made a mistake. He had taken Anne's empty words of kindness as genuine concern. He felt like the fool they both thought he was for appealing to them.

Quick anger reared up and coiled inside him.

His shoulders swayed as he clenched and unclenched his fists. Poised to strike, he stepped forward.

'No, not like this,' shouted a voice inside his head. 'Starting a fight will get you nowhere.'

Jimmy halted; stood locked his footsteps.

A fight is what they want he told himself. It would give them an excuse to have him arrested.

No way.

He wouldn't play into their hands. "I offered Lori a ride," he spat in his own defense. "Had she accepted it I would've taken her home. The opportunity to kill her would've been lost and she would still be alive."

"Jimmy . . ." Anne struggled to find her voice, "Are you saying you killed Lori because she wouldn't accept a ride with you?"

Frustrated, he shook his head. His gaze dropped to the porch floor. Jimmy watched a tree beetle skitter across the gray painted surface. It took cover from the light beneath a fallen maple leaf.

Jimmy wished he could crawl under something and hide just as the beetle had, and never face the world again. Greg and Anne had misunderstood what he'd said. He wished that his words had come out better. Now the Johnson's had drawn the wrong conclusion.

Even so, when Jimmy spoke again he couldn't hide the bitterness in his tone. "I can't trust anybody in this damned town. I came here because I thought you meant what you said at the picnic. Because no woman in town will have anything to do with me, Tate says I scatter tacks and nails along the roads then drive around all night looking for stranded women I can rape and murder.

"I once found a tack on the service station floor near the Coke machine, one just like what drivers pick up in their tires on the road. Sheriff Tate was the only person who'd been inside the station that morning. The tack must've fallen from his pocket when he pulled out change for a Coke.

"Tate drops those tacks on the road so people can't drive up on him the nights he rides horseback naked. I work day and night because I have nothing else to do. No woman will date me and I have no male friends. I work and make money I don't need just to stay busy."

"Jimmy . . ." tears swelled in Anne's eyes, "I have never believed you murdered those women. I've always wanted to hear your side of the story. But it sounds like you're confessing to the murders."

"Jimmy, come inside," Greg unlocked the screen door and held it open, "We want to hear everything you can tell us about the murders and what you want from us." Although visibly shaken, Greg's tone remained calm. "You should've sought us out sooner."

Greg and Anne led him to the dining room and showed him a seat at a big round table. "I'll make some coffee." Anne disappeared.

Afraid that she had gone to call Tate, Jimmy started to bolt but decided he'd have his say before he took off running. It would be a while before Tate got there and understood what was going on. By then Jimmy would be halfway across the county. Maybe what he said now would sink into somebody's head later.

"When I get tired of driving, I pull off Old Mill Road, take a leak, and then listen to the night calls mingle with my CD music. The different insects singing background makes it sound even prettier.

"Most times though, I just fall asleep.

"Twice in two different locations, something that sounded like pleading woke me up. I left the truck and crept through the weeds to see what was going on. Both times, I saw a woman running.

"The first woman, Amy Snodgrass was so close when she ran past me I could've reached out and pulled her into the bushes. I decided not to because it would scare her too much.

"Before I could do anything, a man holding a knife ran up and attacked her—"

Anne's stunned gasp signaled her return. Along with the coffee, she carried three slices of coconut cake Jimmy recognized as the same he'd enjoyed at the picnic.

"Jimmy we thought you were confessing to the

murders."

He shook his head hoping he didn't look as miserable as he felt. "I would never hurt a woman. Three murders have happened right before my eyes. Each time including tonight, it was the same killer."

Jimmy couldn't resist sinking a fork into the cake then shoveling a chunk of it into his mouth. He'd forgotten until now that he'd missed dinner. "Until tonight, I couldn't prove I'd seen the murders," he said between bites. "No one would've believed me anyway. Everybody swears I did it."

Jimmy fell silent. He ran his hands up and down his arms, massaging the tight muscles. His arms ached the way they did when he got cold in the winter. He knew the pain was due in part to the trouble he faced and recognition of his own shortcomings. He hated that he hadn't thought before tonight to grab the cell phone to take pictures. He regretted that he hadn't pulled out a wrench to use as a weapon before he went to investigate the disturbances, but fights and spats were common along that road.

He seldom got any personal calls on the cell and took it along only when he knew he would tow a vehicle. He carried guns only when he went hunting.

"Cecil Jones once cheated me out of some money the county owed me. He claimed I'd dented some county vehicles. I had my phone tonight so no one could say I'd damaged an expensive car. I had the cell in my hand to loan it to Lori if she still refused to accept a ride."

"I recall hearing something about the Cecil Jones thing," Greg said.

"Cecil lied. I think he found a way to pocket the money. Maybe I shouldn't stay mad about it. Maybe I should thank him instead. His lie taught me to protect myself by photographing the fronts and rear ends of vehicles before and after I tow them." Jimmy then explained why he had been on Old Mill Road earlier and how he had come to witness Lori's death. As he talked, he pulled the cell phone from his pocket.

"On here, the dated and time-stamped pictures show Lori's disabled car. Other pictures I took tonight explain how things happened." Jimmy slid Greg the phone across the table. "The hooked up rear end of Jared's car and where it's parked proves I went there to tow it. The next one shows it unhooked which says I left it where it set undamaged then went off to clear the accident.

"The killer waited out of sight halfway down the gorge in case somebody drove past. When the pines brush against each other, they make peculiar swishing sounds that muffle the road noises. He didn't hear me drive up. You can see only a few feet through the pines during the day, but at night, you can see nothing through the sway. The killer did hear the tires blow out. But by the time he reached the top of the hill to see what had happened, I was gone and Lori was there alone in her car. Since he didn't know I'd been there, he couldn't expect me to double back. He did know that chances were slim anyone would come along.

"The next picture shows Lori's car and the area around it after her murder. The last one," Jimmy couldn't hide his admiring grin, "Is a handsome ten-point buck standing in the parking area above the Leap."

Three hours later, Jimmy had revealed what he knew about the murders. He had answered both Greg's and Anne's questions. Once he had felt certain Tate wasn't coming to arrest him, he had relaxed and decided to face whatever came later. He knew he couldn't run forever. Anne seemed genuinely concerned about him. She'd listened close to what he had said. Judging by her nods and smiles and the left over pot roast she piled high on the plate she set before him, she believed him.

So did Greg.

"Jim, go on home and get some rest. When the investigators end their work, they'll call you to tow the vehicle. Until then that area is on lock down. No one can travel through it."

"I promised Jared Bolton I would pick him up tomorrow morning and drive him to his car."

Greg placed a call to one of the investigators and repeated what Jimmy had said.

"They'll let you drive Jared to his car," Greg said. "A deputy at the road block will give you further instructions."

Filled with a new sense of awareness, Jimmy now strolled for the tow truck. He glanced around him. Everything about he and the night felt alive. An evening-cooled breeze winged in on pine-scented air. Somewhere on a distant street, a dog yapped excited about something. Jimmy felt the tenseness in his body relax. Well-being rested on his shoulders. In the past few hours, his life had taken a sudden upswing. His feet, instead of plodding with rejection, now stepped sprightly.

Jimmy inhaled deep, released, and then inhaled again. Each intake of breath, inflated a swell of promise in his chest. The peace and respect he had longed for all his life now loomed a certainty before him.

Greg had consulted county officials by e-mail and by phone. He'd sent them copies of the photos Jimmy took. Pine Ridge Homicide Investigators had already visited the murder scene. They had verified that a homicide had indeed taken place there and investigation into it was underway.

CHAPTER TWELVE

Jared Bolton lived on the corner of Spruce and Loblolly in a new section of Pine Hollow where most Hamilton Mills executives lived. Expansive two and three-story brick homes, each one outshining the other, towered above rambling lawns.

Jimmy neared Jared's driveway at seven, the time of morning when daylight peeked above the pines, the time of morning when birds greeted the new day.

Through the open truck window, Jimmy heard their chatter; witnessed a kamikaze blue jay dive to the pavement in front of the truck, grab a beetle then clear the wheels by a hair on its feathers. Grey doves stood in the center of a three-tiered birdbath on Jared's lawn flapping water over their feathers.

Jimmy yawned wide. He wondered why Jared, a single man needed so much house and yard and why he was leaving home at seven when the race didn't start 'til nine.

The moment Jimmy turned into the drive Jared headed toward the truck. Dressed in white running shorts and a tee shirt he had stood outside on the walk near the wide circling front porch. He climbed in the truck, settled on the seat, and then reached over and pumped Jimmy's right shoulder.

"Good morning. Jimmy, perfect timing I just stepped out the door. Looks like a great day for the run. The forecast says clear and sunny. Have you ever thought about joining us sometime? I'll gladly give you some pointers that will help you prepare for it."

Disinterested Jimmy muttered, "Too busy. I've decided to start working out."

Right now, he knew he was too tired to think much about anything. Last night, he'd tossed unable to sleep for thinking about Lori. Once he drifted off, the phone woke him up. Greg was asking if Jimmy had seen a third vehicle stranded on Old Mill Road. Greg said Pine Ridge officials had received a report that Beth Hines hadn't arrived home following the Pine Hollow picnic. No one she knew in either town had seen her. The investigators had learned that she and Lori had once been close friends, but a romantic rivalry had ended that friendship. The investigators asked if he could offer any insight into her whereabouts.

He hadn't seen Beth or her car on the road last night he told Greg. At the same time, Jimmy couldn't help but think that Beth had snuck off somewhere and didn't want anyone to find her. He had just gotten back to sleep when a five a.m., call asked him to tow a vehicle.

"If you change your mind," Jared said, "Let me know. Do me a favor; stop at the convenience store on the corner so I can grab us some coffee and a newspaper for the ride to the car."

Five minutes later, Jimmy turned right on Old Mill Road. As soon as Jared returned with the coffees, he hid behind the newspaper.

As Jimmy neared Lovers Leap, patches of morning mist hung in the forest air. He wondered if the authorities had told Sheriff Tate and Deputy Weston the county was launching an investigation into their conduct on and off patrol. Last night, Jimmy had overheard Greg tell someone on the phone that the authorities would advise Buzz and Tate when they arrived for work this morning.

Buzz won't take it without a fight, thought Jimmy. Buzz thought he was God's gift to law enforcement and nobody should question his judgment . . .

Jimmy lifted his foot off the accelerator; let the truck slow . . .

Ahead, a county vehicle flashing emergency lights blocked the road. Buzz stood outside the cruiser turning drivers back to town. Puzzled, Jimmy wondered how Buzz had gotten there so fast. Less than fifteen minutes ago, Jimmy had passed Buzz's house. The place was dark and the cruiser stood parked in the driveway.

Buzz saw the tow truck approaching and hurried toward it. One hand near his holster: "Raise your hands in the air and get out of the truck," Buzz trained his eyes on Jimmy.

"What the hell's going on?" Jimmy asked. "I'm driving Jared to his car."

"Get out of the truck with your hands raised," Buzz repeated. This time he jerked the revolver from the holster.

"What's the problem, officer," Jared lowered the paper.

"This is none of your concern. Put your hands on the dashboard where I can see them and stay inside the truck," Buzz answered.

Hands raised, Jimmy stepped to the pavement.

His anger instantly rose.

Old misgivings rushed back. A sudden sick sensation twisted in the pit of his stomach. He'd walked into a trap. Anne and Greg had screwed him royally.

His thoughts spinning Jimmy searched his mind for a way out. He had kicked Buzz's ass twice years ago. Later Buzz and his family had left town. One swift punch now would lay him out cold before his fingers curled around the trigger. Then Jimmy would . . .

Just then, Dispatcher Rhodes' voice sounded on the patrol car radio: "Deputy Weston, when the tow truck shows up at the roadblock, have Cooper head straight past Dead Man's Curve. Tell him no stops along the way. They need an immediate tow so they can release the scene."

"I'm about to cuff him and put him under arrest."

"Hang on. I'll get right back," Dispatcher Rhodes said.

Seconds later, Rhodes returned. "Sheriff Tate says let Cooper through or you'll be arrested."

Resisting the urge to bombard Buzz with the choice cuss words he reserved just for him, Jimmy grinned instead, "Barney Fife." Back on the road he snaked the speeding truck around the curves headed for the murder scene.

Jared's white-knuckled right fingers clutched the right armrest. His left hand braced against the dashboard. The newspaper on his lap slid to the floor. Fear clouded his eyes as the tow truck careened past Lovers Leap. "What's going on? Why the road block?" Jared asked. "I need to get to the race."

"Another serial killing," Jimmy tersely replied.

Jimmy slowed only when he neared the Pine Hollow and Pine Ridge officials standing near the road. He drove past county cars and emergency vehicles parked along both sides of the highway. A short distance ahead, the Pine Ridge coroner's van pulled from the overgrowth.

Sleep well, Lori, Jimmy whispered a mental goodbye. He knew the Medical Examiner's van would transport her body to the Pine Ridge Pathology Center. Holding back tears, Jimmy crept past Lori's disabled car then backed up and aligned the tow truck with its rear. As he always did when Dispatch called him for a law enforcement tow, he remained inside the truck awaiting further instructions.

Moments later, a tall gray-haired detective, Dan Russell from the Pine Ridge office, walked over. Jimmy recognized him from the other homicide scenes.

"James Cooper?"

"Yes," Jimmy acknowledged.

"And you are," Russell eyed Jared.

"Jared Bolton"

"I'm Detective Dan Russell. Do you know a Beth Hines?" He spoke directly to Jared.

"Yes, I do. Why has something happened to her?"

"We have a report that she traveled this road last night, but never arrived home after a company picnic."

"She was terrified of being alone on the road because of the killings. I trailed her until I thought she would be safe traveling alone," Jared moved to exit the truck, "I'll begin an immediate search—"

"That won't be necessary just yet," Detective Russell declined Jared's offer. "Mr. Cooper, I believe we've met before. Remain in the truck until I give you the go ahead to move the vehicle. Mr. Bolton, please step outside, stand near your vehicle, and wait. No one can leave until the last deputy arrives and we release control of the scene."

Even as Detective Russell spoke, Buzz sauntered up to where Sheriff Tate stood leaning against a tree. Tate looked as if he would cry.

That Beth hadn't been located took Jimmy by surprise. He'd thought by now she would've turned up at home. Without warning, his emotions got the best of him.

Lori was dead.

Since he hadn't defended her or the other women, the least he could do now was honor her memory. He would put some serious hurt on her killer standing right there with them.

Jimmy reached under the seat and pulled out the heavy crescent wrench he'd shoved under there this morning. He pulled the handle to open the door—

"As most of you know there's been another serial killing," Detective Russell wasted no time stating. "We've identified the deceased as Lori Manning. However, this latest homicide has brought forward an eyewitness. Luckily, the eyewitness recorded what he saw on his cell phone. I've already passed around those cell phone pictures.

"To give you some initial background, tow truck driver, James Cooper arrived here last night to tow that vehicle reported out of gas earlier," Russell nodded first at Jimmy then at the Red Lamborghini.

Jimmy took a deep breath, settled back against the seat deciding for the moment to stay put and watch the killer's reaction.

"The first photo the eyewitness took shows the vehicle hooked up for tow," Dan went on. "The second photo shows the vehicle released in the same spot where it now sets. A second vehicle appeared right after the eyewitness took the first snapshot. You'll notice the second snapshot shows the second vehicle facing the tow truck.

"The third photo captures much of the surrounding area and the second vehicle that arrived on the scene. That vehicle in this photo now faces the opposite direction. Its blown out front tires tell a story.

"The eyewitness shot the third photograph after the homicide happened. That second vehicle remains here now, the front tires damaged. Look again at the third picture then look back at the first and second snapshots.

"Only one vehicle and the back of the tow truck appear in the first photo. Two vehicles and the back of the tow truck show in the second photo. Look again at the third picture. It reveals only one vehicle in the area. The tow truck's gone. So is one of the two vehicles. Unless Cooper towed away a vehicle when he left the scene and for some reason failed to report it, one of those disabled cars left on its own.

"Our witness reports that a vehicle sped past him as he pulled from the overgrowth just moments after the homicide. The fourth shot pictures a ten-point buck in the parking area above Lovers Leap. The eyewitness snapped that shot when he drove past there a few minutes later. He'd just left the homicide scene and was on his way to town."

Jimmy watched as Buzz squatted, grabbed a stick, and

then started doodling in the dirt.

"Earlier," Russell said, "When the eyewitness passed the Leap headed in this direction, the parking area there was vacant—no car—no deer. Right after our office received report of the homicide, an investigator checked the Lovers Leap area. He too found it vacant. Two hours later, a second investigator went to the Leap and discovered a vehicle parked in the space. You don't have a copy, but our investigator took a picture of that parked vehicle.

"At five this morning," Detective Russell went on, "We decided we'd play our own game of disappearing and reappearing vehicles. We went through the vehicle parked at the Leap then had it towed back to its original spot. I believe it's safe to say the whole thing was an elaborate set-up for a homicide.

"Our investigation so far has determined that only someone possessing the keys could've driven the vehicle from the homicide scene; left the area; drove back to the Leap, parked, and then traveled on foot almost five miles back to town. Obviously, the vehicle with the tire damage wasn't the one that left the spot on its own.

"Jared Bolton, your Lamborghini was never out of fuel as you reported it. You drove that vehicle away. Later, you drove back and parked the car at the Leap. You knew everyone would accept your word that the vehicle had set there all night. You felt certain no one had traveled the road and there'd be no dispute to your claim. You believed you'd never be a suspect because everyone knows you frequently run out of gas on the road.

"You never considered the possibility of an eyewitness. And you had no way of knowing that eyewitness would photograph a ten-point buck occupying the spot at the Leap at the time you'd claim your out-of-gas vehicle was parked there.

"You killed Lori Manning and the other four women stranded alone on Old Mill Road and then left their bodies lying like road kill in the overgrowth."

ABOUT THE AUTHOR

Tina Hill is a published author with a variety of online articles and one out-of-print romance novel to her credit. Road Kill is her first venture into eBook publishing and she is currently writing an e-cookbook.